MW00884070

The Barn and the Book

by

Melinda Johnson

ANCIENT FAITH PUBLISHING

Chesterton, Indiana

The Barn and the Book
Text copyright © 2018 Melinda Johnson
Cover and interior illustrations by Clare Freeman

All rights reserved. No part of this publication may be reproduced
by any means, electronic, mechanical, photocopying, recording,
scanning, or otherwise, without the prior written permission of the
publisher.

Published by:
        Ancient Faith Publishing
        A division of Ancient Faith Ministries
        PO Box 748
        Chesterton IN 46304

ISBN: 978-1-944967-43-7

store.ancientfaith.com

We are grateful to the nuns at Holy Transfiguration Monastery in Ellwood City,
PA, for their helpful review of the depictions of nuns in this fictional monastery.

PRINTED IN THE UNITED STATES OF AMERICA

For Majesta, always, and for everyone
who treasures their Christmas memories.

CHAPTER

ONE

WHEN SISTER ANNA made the announcement, Macrina was the only one paying attention. Macrina always paid attention. Grace was secretly playing with a rock under the table, trying to decide if it was a real rock or only a chunk of old concrete. Every other child in the third-and-fourth-grade Sunday school classroom was staring at the long rectangular window along the top of the left-hand wall. The classroom was in the church basement, so the window was near the ceiling. It was clean and bright, like everything at the monastery. Except in one spot.

Saucer the Corgi sat on his haunches on the grass outside the window. His nose was pressed firmly against the glass, and the children inside could see the wet, heart-shaped mark it was making. Little puffs of steamy breath whisked in and out of his nose, dragon style. It was cold outside.

Saucer was staring at Sam, who was sitting just below him on the fourth-grade side of the classroom table. Sam was staring back at Saucer. Whenever Sam came to the Monastery of St. Gerasim, Saucer followed him everywhere he went. Saucer had tried to follow Sam into the classroom, but when that didn't work, he set up camp outside the window and stared at Sam all through class. He sat in the same spot every week, and Sam sat in the same chair inside the classroom, so they were always together. Saucer bounced sideways every few minutes as if he were going to run away, but he wouldn't leave without Sam.

Sister Anna knew the children weren't paying attention. She wished they would pay attention, but it never surprised her when they didn't. Clasping her dimpled hands together, Sister Anna tried again. "Children? Children, I have something to tell you."

Macrina frowned at her classmates. Elias, Sam, and another fourth-grader on her side of the table were staring at that ridiculous dog. Everyone on the third-grade side was now playing with things under the table. Matthew and his neighbor were hiding a pencil duel under there, and Grace was staring intently at her hand, which probably meant she'd brought another rock to class.

"Ahem!" said Macrina loudly.

Sister Anna flinched. "I know you're all thinking about Christmas coming, but I want you to look ahead to springtime for a few minutes. The monastery will celebrate its one hundredth birthday on March fourth, which is Saint Gerasim's feast day and our name day."

Macrina nodded encouragingly.

Grace suddenly looked up from her rock. "Do you get presents from Saint Nicholas here? We did that at my old church, before we moved."

"We're not talking about that right now," said Macrina. "Let Sister Anna finish talking. She's going to tell us something."

"Yes, that's right, dear," said Sister Anna, regaining control of the conversation. "We're going to celebrate our one hundredth anniversary, and we will be printing a commemorative book, for the celebration. Sister Sophia and Sister Katherine will put in pictures and letters from the archives and write about the history of the monastery. But we'd like to also include something from you children. Not every monastery is lucky enough to have a Sunday school class like we do. But that's the bright side of being the only Orthodox church in this county!" She paused. "I wish we could put in something from all of you, and maybe we can, but you would all have to do it together—"

Macrina shook her head vigorously. Her long black braid slipped over her shoulder and she flipped it back, frowning so hard that her eyebrows ran into each other in the middle of her forehead.

"—because there's only room in the book for one or maybe two pages from you children. Books are expensive to print," explained Sister Anna apologetically.

Elias had been paying attention every few seconds, between thinking about something else. His straw-colored hair stood up like a brush. His white button-down shirt was coming untucked as he slouched in the folding chair. He thought he heard the word "birthday" and then "only one." His gray eyes came into focus.

"Only one what?" asked Elias.

"One story. It will be a beautiful book, but not large. We have room for one story, or an essay, written by you children. You can do it together, or you can each try writing something and let us choose." Sister Anna paused. Her black robe rustled as she reclasped her hands. "Even if your story isn't chosen for the book, we will make copies of it to share with our guests at the celebration."

Grace put the rock into her skirt pocket and looked up. "What celebration?"

Sister Anna opened her mouth, but Macrina was faster.

"Are *any* of you paying attention? Sister Anna just told us it's the monastery's one hundredth birthday in March, and we're going to spend the whole winter getting ready. There's a book! If you write something good enough, it can be in the book. Don't you want to be *published*?"

Sister Anna began squeezing her hands together, over and over again. It looked like she was kneading a tiny loaf of bread between her palms. "It's not quite being published, Macrina. There will just be copies printed for our guests and our friends."

"But it will be in the monastery bookstore, won't it?" asked Macrina.

"Yes, dear. That's true."

"Well, that's the same as being published. I'm going to write something."

"Me too! I'm going to write something." Grace lunged to her feet and started toward the craft table where the paper and pencils were kept. "I can think of ten hundred things to write!"

"But only one of our stories can go in the book,"
began Macrina.

"So what?" Elias grinned at her. "So you think no
one else should even try just because you want to do it?"

"Children," squeaked Sister Anna. "This is not the
point. It's not a competition. The book is meant to be a
record of the monastery's history and to give examples of
the beautiful community we are blessed to have around
us here."

"It is too a competition," Sam spoke up suddenly.
Outside the window, Saucer jumped up and pawed the
glass. "If only one person gets in the book, they have to
beat out everyone else."

"Oh, no. Oh, dear me." Sister Anna's shoulders

drooped. Her habit suddenly looked too big for her.

Macrina swiveled around in her chair and stared at Grace, who was scrabbling through the basket on the craft table, looking for her favorite pencil. "What are you going to write about?"

Grace stared back, round-eyed. "I'm not going to tell."

Macrina snorted. "I'm not going to steal your idea! I have my own idea."

"And you think it's better than hers," said Elias. "Huh. You're so obvious, Macrina."

Macrina shut her lips tight and folded her hands in her lap. She was certainly not going to squabble in front of a nun.

Sam got up. "I need to take Saucer for a walk."

Saucer was bounding back and forth on his short legs, rolling his eyes and flinging up his nose to yowl at the sky.

"You go ahead, dear," said Sister Anna, relieved to be able to approve of something.

Sam pushed back his chair. He bumped into three other children and a bookcase on his way out the door, but his classmates paid no attention to him. Everyone knew that Sam could go with Saucer whenever he wanted to. They were more interested in the fight starting up between Macrina and Grace.

Sister Anna gazed at the room full of children. Grace stood by the craft table, ripping the paper off a crayon. Beside her, Elias had leaned back in his chair and folded his arms on his chest. Macrina's nose was in the air.

"Well, that's all for today," said Sister Anna as brightly as she could. "Let's go upstairs and find our families, shall we?"

For a second, no one moved. The argument wasn't over. Sister Anna should solve things before the class left.

"Off you go," said Sister Anna, waving her hands at the children. She turned her back and began erasing the whiteboard behind her. Reluctantly, the children pushed back their chairs and left the classroom. She could hear them running toward the stairs at the end of the hall. Sister Anna rested her forehead on the board and sighed.

In the hall, Elias caught up with Macrina. "You could write something together," he began. "You could even organize it. You could get Grace and maybe some other kids who—"

"No," hissed Macrina.

"Why do you always have to fight about everything?" growled Elias.

"I don't fight about anything at all! Fighting is wrong." Macrina flipped her braid over her shoulder.

"Huh. You're fighting with me right now," countered Elias.

Macrina stopped walking and whirled around, hands on her hips. "No, *you're* fighting with *me*."

"You're fighting with me about not fighting with me." Elias put his hands on his hips, copying her.

Macrina blew all the air out of her lungs, rolled her eyes, and started walking again.

Matthew, who was coming back from the stairs to find his older brother, had to jump sideways into the wall to avoid being run down by Macrina.

"What's wrong with her?" asked Matthew.

"Who knows?" said Elias. "Did you find Mom and Dad? Can we go now?"

"They're upstairs talking to Sam's parents and whoever else, but Dad said for me to come find you."

"Well, you found me, so let's go."

CHAPTER

TWO

SISTER ANNA washed the whiteboard and walked around the classroom, pushing in chairs and picking up stray pencils from under the table. Then she turned out the lights and closed the classroom door.

The hall was empty now. She could hear the voices of nuns and families visiting together upstairs. Sister Anna tiptoed to the other end of the hall, climbed a smaller staircase, and let herself out the door at the top.

Sister Anna was too short and pudgy to move quickly, but she did her best. She wanted to reach the prayer garden without being seen. It was too cold to sit there for long, but Sister Anna needed some quiet time.

When she reached the prayer garden, she sat down on her favorite seat in her favorite corner. The seat was an old tree stump that had been made into a low-backed chair beside a sheltering box hedge and a flower garden. The seat was just right for Sister Anna; it wasn't very tall, and neither was she.

Sister Anna's round face peered out at the world from the plain black wrapping of her habit. She loved her habit. It clothed her and kept her warm, and she felt that it hid her from the world. The monastery was a world away from the world, and Sister Anna in her black robe was a smaller world within that smaller world.

For a few moments, she sat still, remembering the spicy summer fragrance of box hedge and blossom now gone from the wintery garden. Frost glistened on the tiny mounds of earth where the flowers had been. Cold air stung her face and fingers. Sister Anna folded her hands and closed her eyes.

Dear Lord Jesus, she whispered, *what shall I do? The children are already fighting over the monastery celebration book. It's completely contrary to the spirit of the project. How can I have let that happen? I wish Gerontissa had asked Sister Katherine to tell them. Sister Katherine puts things so well. She says "here's what we'll do," and then people do it. I wish I had that gift.*

Sister Anna stopped praying and thought about Sister Katherine. Sister Katherine was very tall, with long hands and feet and a face that was always smiling. Sister Anna had been at the monastery for five years, just like Sister Katherine, but somehow, Sister Anna always thought of her as an authority. Even the goats and the ducks did what Sister Katherine told them to do. She never raised her voice or lost her patience or paused to be confused. She smiled and explained clearly and went forward confidently in faith.

Sister Anna sighed.

Lord Jesus Christ, Son of God, have mercy on me, a sinner. I want to bring peace, Lord, but I don't bring peace. I want to do Your will, but the more I try to see what it is, the more I don't see what it is. I try to make myself small so You can be great, but all I do is make myself so small that I can't get anything done.

Sister Anna felt her prayer had reached a dead end. She was just going to say "Amen" when she heard a scuffling sound. She opened her eyes with the word unsaid.

Grace stood a few feet away on the other side of the empty flower bed. Bright red beads sparkled at the tips of her braids, and her brown eyes were round and shining. When Sister Anna's eyes opened, Grace waved to her with one hand. The other hand was cupped carefully around a rock. Sister Anna hadn't known Grace long, but she had never seen her without a rock in her hand.

"Hi, Sister Anna! Were you praying? I always wanted to see a real nun praying. Macrina says she sees nuns praying all the time, but I just moved to this town, so I never saw one yet."

Sister Anna closed her eyes again, said "Amen" very quickly, and opened them. "Hello, Grace."

"Do you want to see my rock?" Grace left the path and scampered straight through the flower bed, hopping and sliding over the rumpled earth. "It has sparkles in it. Maybe it's gold!"

Sister Anna peered into the grimy palm held up to

her and saw a gray rock with flecks of mica in it.

"That's a nice rock. Do you collect them?"

"Yes, I always collect the pretty ones. I might be a geologist when I grow up." Grace dropped the rock into her pocket. "Also, I might be a farmer, because I really like goats. The best day ever would be if I found a golden rock *and* got to play with a goat. Macrina says you have goats here." Grace smiled hopefully at Sister Anna.

"Yes, dear, we have goats." Sister Anna stood up. "You know, I like the goats, too. They're very energetic. They talk to each other all day, and they hop around in their pen."

"Can we go see them?" asked Grace, hopping from one foot to the other.

"Well . . ." Sister Anna hesitated. "Well, I think we

should go find your family, but we could walk past the animal farm on the way if you like."

Grace squeaked with joy and raced across the frosty grass toward the path.

"Grace, wait!" cried Sister Anna, trotting after her and clutching her skirt to keep from tripping on it. "You don't know which way to go."

"It's okay!" shouted Grace over her shoulder. "I'll just keep going round and round until I see a goat!"

Sister Anna nodded to herself. No one could be lost at the monastery. A single path ran from the church on its low hill to the door of every building and the edge of every garden. Grace would find the goats, or anything else she was seeking, if she simply followed the path.

Sister Anna walked as fast as her short legs would

let her. Her black habit whipped back and forth as she struggled to keep up with Grace. Grace ran straight down the path at full speed. Her beaded braids swung and sparkled, making a sound like castanets. Her knee socks slid down around her ankles. Her unzipped coat streamed behind her.

"Hooray!" shouted Grace. "We're going to see the goats!"

Sister Anna heard barking up ahead. As they rounded the bend in the path, she saw Sam and Saucer playing by the gate of the animal farm. Sam looked happy and relaxed. Although she was out of breath, Sister Anna smiled. Sam and Saucer were best friends.

Sam looked up as Grace skidded to a stop in front of him. "What are you doing?"

"Goats!" cried Grace, waving her arms. "I'm here to

see goats!" She skipped around him to the gate and clambered up on the cross bar. "Are they in here?"

"Yes," said Sam, getting to his feet. Saucer bounced over to the gate. "Look in there, to the left."

Grace leaned over the gate, locking her knees and clutching the top rail to keep her balance. "I see another dog and a chicken, too! Are those ducks or geese? Is that a donkey? It's a whole farm! There should be a cow!"

By this time, Sister Anna had arrived. "Grace, dear, if you step down, we can open the gate."

Grace jumped down, and Sister Anna reached for the latch.

Saucer barked. He galloped around Sam and Grace, and sat down firmly on Sister Anna's feet.

"Oh, dear." Sister Anna clasped her hands. "Up, Saucer. Can you get up?"

Saucer got up, took a large mouthful of Sister Anna's skirt, and braced his front paws on the ground, pulling her away from the gate. Sister Anna staggered backward and grasped the fence to keep her balance. Saucer let go of her skirt and sat down on her feet again, finishing the job. Grace giggled.

"It's because you aren't Sister Katherine," explained Sam gruffly. "He won't let you in because he knows it's her farm."

"It's everybody's farm, dear," panted Sister Anna, shuffling her feet out from under Saucer. As soon as she stepped back, Saucer hopped up and sat down on her feet again. "Oh, dear! Maybe I should go get Sister Katherine."

"It's okay," said Sam. "I can let you in."

"You can?"

"Saucer trusts me," said Sam proudly.

Sister Anna's shoulders drooped. "I don't think he trusts me."

"Don't feel bad," chirped Grace, hopping down off the gate. "We're going to see goats!"

"Saucer, come!" said Sam firmly.

Saucer's ears twitched.

"Come!"

Saucer fixed his bright black eyes on Sister Anna's face and held his ground for several seconds more. Then he stood up slowly, snuffed loudly, and bounced over to the gate, rearing up on his back legs to rest his paws on the crossbar.

"That's right, Saucer," said Sam, coming over to pat the fuzzy spot between Saucer's pointed ears. "Now back up so we can get in already."

Saucer barked, but he dropped down onto the ground and sat back on his haunches next to Sam.

"Thank you, Saucer," said Sister Anna with a sigh of relief.

Saucer grinned at her and let his tongue loll out of his mouth.

Sam lifted the latch, and the gate squeaked open.

Squeeeak . . . click.

The animals inside the little farm stopped doing whatever they had been doing and all started talking at once.

"Baaaa! Baaaaaa! Quack! Quack! Hee-haw! Buk-buk! Woof!"

"You could oil that gate," said Grace to Sister Anna. "You could oil the squeak."

"No, don't." Sam shook his head. "I like it that way."

Sister Anna stood to one side, holding the gate open. Saucer trotted in and paused at his square, red dog house to lap up a drink from his water bowl. Sam followed him and stood still, watching him drink before following Grace down to the goat pen.

Grace ran through the gate and galloped along the dirt path, waving and calling to every animal she passed. The goats, always excited by the presence of nuns and other humans, surged toward the inner side of their pen, bleating loudly and frolicking.

Grace stopped so suddenly that Sam and Saucer nearly piled up on top of her. She crouched on the path. "I saw a sparkly rock!" Her fingers scrabbled against the packed dirt of the path. A small flat rock popped out.

"Look!" She held it up.

Sam stared at her.

"That's a nice rock," said Sister Anna. "And look, Grace, there are the goats!"

Sister Anna made her way around Grace to the goat pen and began to pat the head of each goat she could reach.

Grace hopped up and down, doing a joyful dance. "Beautiful goats! So many goats! Maaaaaah! Maaaaaah! I can talk to the goats!"

The goats loved Grace. They plunged back and

forth inside their pen, bleating joyfully and bumping into each other.

"What are their names?" asked Grace, coming to stand next to Sister Anna and pat the goats' noses whenever they came near enough to reach.

"Hop, Skip, Jump, Et Cetera, and So Forth," said Sister Anna. "Hello, nice goats. Hello. Yes, you're a very nice goat. But put your nose back through, nice goat. Sister Katherine will come to feed you later."

Sam watched Sister Anna and Grace enjoying the goats. He wished Grace would hurry up and leave. She wasn't as bad as Macrina, but he liked to have the animal farm to himself. At least she wasn't trying to play with Saucer. Sam crouched down and put his arm around Saucer. Saucer licked Sam's ear.

CHAPTER

THREE

THE PAINTING PROJECT began in the first week of October. All the parents and teenagers brought their oldest clothes to church at the monastery each Sunday. The nuns made soup and bread for lunch, and after lunch, the parents and teenagers spent the afternoon chipping old paint off buildings, sanding rough wood, and applying an undercoat and a top coat of new paint. On cold clear days, they painted outside. When it rained, they painted inside. Everyone wanted the monastery to look its best for the celebration in the spring.

Sister Katherine, who was an excellent planner,

made a diagram that included every building on the monastery grounds, even Saucer's dog house. She drew a neat square or rectangle to show the location of each building, and each of these shapes had a checklist of tasks next to it in small, neat handwriting. The checklist said:

❑ Chip paint

❑ Sand and clean

❑ Primer

❑ First coat

❑ Second coat

❑ Finish

Each item on the list had a tiny box next to it, and Sister Katherine made a tiny check in the tiny box each time a task was completed. The diagram was posted in the monastery office, and Sister Anna gazed at it reverently every time she came to the office. It was miraculous to her.

Sister Katherine had not left out a single building. Sister Katherine had not forgotten a single task. All the words were spelled correctly, and the check boxes were so tiny and so remarkably uniform in shape and perfect in size.

Every Sunday, Grace tried to join the team of grownups and older kids so she could paint a building. She loved paint! She loved the heavy wooden brushes with their smooth, flexible bristles. She loved the thick, creamy paint. She loved the wet, ploppy sound of paint slapping against wood and soaking into all its pores and creases.

"No, dear," said Grace's mother, every Sunday. "Sister Katherine only has enough brushes and paint pots for the grownups to use. The best help you children can give us is to play happily together while we get this work done."

"Couldn't I paint just a little bit?" pleaded Grace. "I could share with you."

"I know, love, but this is a big job, and we only have a few months to get it done. All of your new friends are here. Use this time to get to know them better."

Grace's mother turned her head back and forth, searching for Grace's new friends. She looked almost exactly like Grace, only bigger. Her black hair was beautifully braided, her face was round and hopeful, and although she didn't carry rocks in her pockets everywhere she went, it wasn't hard to imagine that she might have done that, when she was younger.

Grace sighed. Her chin sank to her chest, and she was about to explain to her mother that she *really, really* wanted to paint when her eye caught a glimmer of something shiny on the ground not far from her feet.

A golden rock? No! A bracelet! Was it a bracelet?

Grace leaned over. It was a bracelet. There weren't any jewels on it. Just round wooden beads and a shiny silver cross. Maybe it belonged to a nun?

"Look," said Grace's mother, who hadn't noticed the bracelet. "There's Macrina. You could play with her, honey. It's so nice to have a girl next door, now that we're in our new house."

Grace looked up. "I found a bracelet, Mama. Can I keep it?"

"Oh, it's someone's prayer beads. See if you can find out who lost it. Ask the other kids. Maybe it belongs to one of them. It will give you something to do while I paint the monastery with Daddy."

Grace's mother gave her a quick hug and walked away. Grace tucked the bracelet into her pocket and set off joyfully. Next to finding goats or golden rocks, going on a mission was Grace's favorite thing to do.

Macrina came along the path toward Grace. She wore a long wool coat buttoned up to her chin, and she carried a notebook and pencil. Grace thought there was something funny about the way Macrina walked. She placed her feet so carefully and held herself so straight. Grace wondered if Macrina was telling herself a story in her head and secretly acting it out as she walked along.

"Hi, Macrina," chirped Grace, juggling the bracelet in her gloved hand. "Is this yours?"

"Oh, hello, Grace." Macrina kept walking.

Grace tried again. "Is this yours?" She held up the bracelet.

Macrina glanced at it over her shoulder. "No, it's not."

"Are you painting?" called Grace to Macrina's back.

Macrina stopped. "No, only the adults are painting."

Grace nodded.

"Besides, I have work to do," said Macrina, tightening her hold on the notebook.

"Your story!" Grace's eyes widened. "I forgot I have to write my story, too."

Macrina shrugged.

"Can I come with you?"

"No, I want to work by myself." Macrina started walking again.

Grace watched her go. Macrina's one long braid twitched importantly with every step. Grace sighed gustily. She turned and was about to start down the path toward the refectory when she had an idea.

I could spy on Macrina, she thought gleefully. *I could hide in the bushes and see what she does!*

Grace waited a few more seconds until Macrina reached a bend in the path. Then she skidded across the frosty grass and flopped down beside a large bush. She peered through the pricker-spiked branches and saw Macrina, still walking along the path with her nose in the air. Grace was sure she was talking to herself.

Grace counted to three and stood up. She picked out another bush on the other side of the path, just a little farther on. Macrina was still walking. Grace charged across the path and flung herself down behind her chosen bush. This one had only a few spindly branches. It was not a good hiding place.

Grace sneezed. It was an unexpected sneeze, and very loud.

Down the path, Macrina lifted her head. Her steps slowed. Grace flattened herself on the ground and closed her eyes tight. For some reason, she always felt more invisible with her eyes closed.

"Grace! Stop following me! I told you I wanted to go by myself."

Grace opened one eye. Macrina's shiny black boots were only a few inches from her face. Before she could think of what a spy should say if the enemy caught her, Grace heard another voice.

"What are you guys doing? Is that Grace under a bush?"

Grace opened her other eye and saw Elias coming

up the path.

"Yes, it's Grace under a bush, and she's following me when I told her not to," said Macrina, disgustedly.

"Hi, Grace," said Elias.

"Goodbye, both of you," said Macrina firmly, and she flounced away down the path again.

"What's with her?" asked Elias.

Grace rolled over and stood up. "I just wanted to see her write her story."

"You don't know Macrina," retorted Elias, grinning.

"My mom keeps telling me to play with her."

"Why?"

Grace hitched up her sock. "Because we moved here this summer, and Macrina lives next door to our new house."

Elias looked at her, considering. "I don't know. You seem pretty different from Macrina."

Grace smiled at him. "Look, I found a bracelet. Is it yours?"

Elias held out his hand, and Grace dropped the bracelet into it. "I think it's Matthew's. Where did you find it?"

"It was on the grass back there." Grace pointed vaguely over her shoulder. "We could go give it to him."

"Sure, why not?" Elias stuffed the bracelet in his coat pocket and started down the path, with Grace walking beside him.

"Don't let Macrina discourage you about your story," said Elias suddenly. "She's always trying to boss everyone, but she's not in charge. If you want to write a story for the book, you should write it."

"Are you going to write one?" asked Grace.

"Maybe," said Elias. "I think some other kids are, too."

"Macrina will probably win," sighed Grace. "She's older than me."

"Yeah, but she's not the judge," Elias reminded her. "The nuns get to pick whose story goes in the book. Just because Macrina thinks she's better than you doesn't mean the nuns agree with her."

"Do the nuns like me?" wondered Grace.

"Sure they do," said Elias, grinning. "Nuns like everybody."

"Everybody?"

Elias nodded. "The nuns even like Macrina," he said impressively.

CHAPTER

FOUR

SAUCER WAS VERY GOOD at paying attention. When Saucer paid attention to anything, he stood perfectly still, staring intently, nose flaring, ears pointing forward as if he were beaming out corgi brainwaves. When Saucer stared at Sam like this, Sam almost felt like Saucer could read his thoughts.

"That dog stares at you a lot. Does he think you're going to give him a treat?" asked Matthew, perched on the log fence that encircled the animal farm.

Sam grunted. He was sitting on the ground inside the fence, next to Saucer's red doghouse.

"I mean, look at him," said Matthew. "If you even move a finger, he twitches his head the same direction."

Sam grinned suddenly and pulled off his mittens. He wiggled a finger. Saucer's eyes flicked after it. His nose twitched. Sam wiggled a finger on his other hand. Saucer's whole head twitched. He raised a front paw.

Matthew slid backwards, hanging by his knees from the fence. "Worrrld uuuuppppsiiiide dOWWWWn!" He laughed and crossed his eyes as the blood rushed to his face. "OOOF!" He hoisted himself back up.

Saucer and Sam looked at each other. Saucer threw up his nose and yowled.

Both boys laughed.

"It's almost like he's human," said Matthew, regaining his seat on top of the fence. "He looks like he could talk."

"I don't need him to talk," said Sam. He patted the furry spot between Saucer's pointed ears. Saucer turned his head to lick Sam's face.

"That dog loves you," said Matthew. "But still, wouldn't it be cool if he could talk?"

"I guess," said Sam. "I already know what he's saying."

"Would it sound like barking?" wondered Matthew. He tried it out in a barky sort of voice. "Arf! I'm Sauc-arf the dog-arf!"

Sam rolled his eyes. Saucer barked.

"See? He knows I'm talking about him!" Matthew slid off the fence and reached a hand to pat Saucer. Saucer flipped his head and sniffed Matthew's hand instead.

"You have to give him your hand to smell first," Sam explained. "Don't just reach for his head like that."

Matthew crouched on the ground and leaned his back against the fence. "Elias says the animals can talk at midnight on Christmas Eve."

Sam snorted.

"For real! He says it happens every year. For one hour, at midnight."

"Where did he get that story?"

"It's a miracle," said Matthew. "He heard it someplace at church, I think. Or maybe not at church. In a book? I don't know. But it's true!"

Sam looked at Saucer. Saucer snuffed and let his tongue hang out. "How do you know it's true?" asked Sam.

"Well, I never heard the animals talk, but you can look it up. There are books and stuff, so somebody must have heard them. It's because Christ was born."

Sam frowned. He didn't know much about Christ being born, but he knew it was a big deal.

Matthew saw the frown. "Do you think it couldn't happen? Miracles can happen! The sisters talk about miracles all over the place."

Sam had been coming to the monastery for less than a year, but even he had heard the sisters talking about miracles.

"Did the sisters ever see any?" he asked.

Matthew stood up. "Of course they did! They're nuns!"

Sam had a vague feeling that this was a good point.

Matthew stood up. "Here comes Elias with Grace." He clambered over the fence and ran down the path toward his older brother. Sam watched Grace and Elias talk to Matthew. Elias dug something out of his pocket and Matthew reached out his hand for it. They talked for a few minutes, and Grace skipped around them, interrupting. Then Elias looked over his shoulder and all three children ran down the path toward Sam.

"It's true, Sam," said Elias, as they reached the gate of the animal farm. "Matthew says he told you about the animals at midnight on Christmas Eve."

"I want to hear them!" shrieked Grace. "I have so many questions! I want to talk to the goats, and the bunnies, and the donkey. What do you think they would say? Does it mean we can hear them, or just that they can talk? Could even beetles talk, or worms?"

"Well," said Elias, considering, "I don't know about beetles and worms, but maybe. Probably anything with a mouth."

Grace was enchanted. "I'm going to stay up on Christmas Eve with a beetle and see if it can talk! I could interview a beetle, or a goat, and write my story for the book about what it said."

Elias grinned at her. "That would be cool," he agreed. He turned to his brother. "Come on, Matthew. Let's go find Mom. If they don't get done painting pretty soon, I'm going to miss my soccer game."

The brothers started down the path. Grace stayed where she was, watching Sam and Saucer.

"That's a nice dog," said Grace, coming closer to the gate.

"Mm-hm," said Sam, keeping his eyes on Saucer.

Grace stepped onto the bottom rail of the fence and rested her elbows on the top rail, gazing at Sam and

Saucer with round, friendly eyes. "Is he your dog?" she asked.

"Sort of," said Sam. "He lives here, but he's mine when I'm here."

"That's the best!" said Grace. "Does he do tricks?"

Sam looked up briefly. "When he wants to."

Grace swung on the gate, tipping her head back and letting the air whisk her braids back and forth. "Maybe Saucer will talk on Christmas Eve. Saucer could talk to you on Christmas Eve, if you were here."

Sam said nothing. He patted Saucer, over and over, and Saucer rested his head on Sam's lap.

"You'll be here. All of us will be," continued Grace. "We'll be here for the service, and then we're going to stay overnight in the guest house. I heard your mom tell my mom."

"I know," said Sam. "Church on Christmas morning."

Grace nodded. "So, we could hear Saucer talk on Christmas Eve!"

Sam looked up. "What do you mean?"

Grace jumped off the gate. "We could stay up. We could come to the animal farm and stay up, and when it was midnight, we would hear the animals talk. Then we would know it was true!"

Sam lowered his head again and went back to patting Saucer. "Maybe."

Grace waited for Sam to say something else, but he didn't. She swung on the gate for a minute more. She wondered if her mother would let her paint if it was just for a few minutes at the very end. Like now, for example. What if she asked her now?

"I'm going to find my mom," she announced. She jumped off the gate and ran down the path, leaving Sam and Saucer alone by the dog house.

Sam sighed. Saucer licked his hand.

"I don't think it's true," said Sam. "But if anyone's going to hear you talk, it's not going to be her."

Saucer barked.

"It's going to be me, Saucer. Don't do it for anyone else, okay?"

CHAPTER

FIVE

"IT'S NOVEMBER FIFTEENTH, children, so today is the first Sunday of the Nativity Fast," began Sister Anna, clasping her hands.

"Look at Saucer!" shrieked someone in the back of the classroom. Every head turned toward the window. Through the frosty glass, the children could see Saucer bouncing back and forth like a ping-pong ball, barking ecstatically.

"Why's he barking?"

"What's he doing, Sam?"

Saucer raced away, disappearing from view as he passed the end of the window.

Sam shoved his chair back and ran to the door.

"Wait!" cried Sister Anna.

Sam didn't wait.

The children leaped out of their seats and ran to the window. It was a high window, at the top of the wall.

"Here!" Elias pushed two chairs over to the wall. Grace grabbed two more chairs and pushed them in front of her, clearing a path through her classmates like a snowplow.

Sister Anna looked around for Macrina. Macrina was always on the side of authority, but Macrina was home with a feverish cold. Sister Anna was on her own. She clasped her hands tighter.

"Children! Please come and sit down. We can find out what happened after class."

Elias jumped up onto a chair. Grace clambered up beside him. Two other children fought off their giggling classmates and managed to climb the other two chairs.

"I can't see!" shouted Grace. "I'm too short! I can't see!"

"What's going on, Elias?" called one of the children who hadn't managed to get up on a chair.

Elias pressed his face flat against the glass and then turned it slightly sideways. He rolled his eyeballs all the way into the corners of his eye sockets. This was a trick he had learned at home, spying on his brother in the back yard. "I see it! I see Sam and Saucer. Oh, wow, I know what happened."

"What? What?" shrieked Grace, grasping the back of her chair and trying to heave it up and down like a pogo stick.

"The goats got out! Well, two of them did. Wow! Look at Saucer go! He's rounding up the goats. It's awesome!" Elias tried to press his face even flatter against the glass.

"Children, come back to your seats, please. Come back!" Sister Anna hurried over to the side of the classroom. "Come off the chairs, children. Somebody could fall and be hurt. Please come back to your seats."

"I'll get down in a minute," promised Grace. "I just want to see Saucer herding the goats!"

Elias jumped down from his chair and beckoned to Grace. "We could see outside. Come on!"

"Oh, yes!" Grace abandoned her chair and headed for the door.

The other children took up the cry. "Come on, come on! Let's go catch some goats!"

Like an ocean wave, the children surged together and flowed out the door in a rush. In seconds, the classroom was empty, and nothing remained but the echo of their footsteps thundering up the stairs.

Sister Anna stood completely still, too stunned to do anything at all.

The clock on the wall behind her ticked through several seconds.

A herd of children raced past the window. She saw their flying feet and heard their laughter faintly through the glass.

A tear rolled down Sister Anna's cheek. She sniffed.

Any minute, the parents of the runaways would realize their children were not in Sunday school. Any minute, Sister Katherine would hear the barking outside and come to help Saucer return the goats to their pen. Any minute, the whole problem would be solved without any help from Sister Anna at all.

Sister Anna bowed her head. Another tear trickled down and dropped onto her habit. Methodically she straightened the table and pulled the chairs back from the window. She picked up scattered pencils and paper, turned the lights off, and closed the classroom door.

Sister Anna climbed the smaller staircase and opened the door at the top. Outside, she heard children's voices and Saucer barking. Peering around the door, she saw Sister Katherine guiding two goats toward the gate of the animal farm. Sam was holding the gate open. Saucer was galloping back and forth behind Sister Katherine, urging the goats to get along home. The rest of the children were perched on the fence or running excitedly in the grass, laughing and cheering.

Sister Anna sniffed again and shut the door behind her. With one last glance to be sure that all of the children were with Sister Katherine, Sister Anna turned away from the church and the animal farm, and made her way to the prayer garden, to her favorite seat in her favorite corner.

Sister Anna sat down slowly. Her breath puffed around her in little clouds. The cold air pressed against her. Sister Anna hugged herself tight for warmth and closed her eyes.

Lord Jesus Christ, Son of God, have mercy on me, a sinner. Lord Jesus Christ, Son of God, have mercy on me, a sinner. Lord Jesus Christ, Son of God, have mercy on me, a sinner.

Sister Anna shivered. She tried to hug herself even tighter.

Oh, Lord Jesus, I made another mistake. I made a big mistake, and that was bad enough, but the big mistake showed me how many other mistakes I'm making. The Sunday school class ran away. The whole class. They ran straight out of the room, and they didn't pay any attention to me at all. They didn't even show that they heard my words. Maybe they didn't. It was so loud in there. But it just shows that my teaching is always bad, not just today. If they had any respect for me, they would listen when I talk. I didn't earn their respect, so now when I need them to listen, they don't.

The air around Sister Anna was completely still. The sounds of the children and Saucer had faded. Perhaps they had gone back into the building.

I shouldn't be the Sunday school teacher. I'm so bad at it. Why did Gerontissa give me this job? It was a mistake.

Sister Anna's eyes popped open. It was hard to imagine Gerontissa—the abbess of the monastery—making a mistake. Maybe it wasn't a mistake. Maybe Gerontissa had some mysterious purpose.

Sister Anna closed her eyes again. *You know I'm not very good at discerning your will, Lord Jesus. I think Gerontissa made a mistake. I think someone else should teach the children. Should I tell her?*

Sister Anna tried to imagine herself seeking out Gerontissa in the small, wood-paneled room behind the monastery office. What would she say to her? Sister Anna realized she would have to begin by explaining that her whole class had escaped from her during Sunday school.

The whole class.

Because of a dog and two runaway goats.

No, not because of goats. Sister Anna closed her eyes again. *Because of me. Because I didn't stop them from running away. I would tell her that, and then she would know that someone else should teach the children. Maybe Sister Sophia. Probably Sister Katherine.*

Sister Anna breathed a long, wobbly sigh in the middle of her prayer. She sat still, squeezing herself and shivering in the cold, cold air.

It's not that I mind telling Gerontissa what happened, Lord. Well, I do mind. But someone else will tell her anyway. Probably, they already have.

Sister Anna let go of herself long enough to bury her face in one hand and shake her head.

In your mercy, Lord Jesus, tell me what to do. Show me a sign.

Her eyes opened again. She was shuddering with cold.

I'm too cold to pray with my eyes shut. Lord, when Gideon wanted a sign that he could truly save Israel from the Midianites, he laid a sheepskin in the grass and came out in the morning to see if it was wet with dew and the ground around it dry. Show me a sign, like Gideon. A sign that will tell me what to do at the monastery. I'm a bad teacher, Lord. But I will ask Gerontissa to help me try again if You want me to. Or I will ask her for another job, if You want me to. How will I know?

Sister Anna stared around the garden, looking for

inspiration. Should she ask for one of the bushes to burst into bloom in the middle of November? That seemed a little over the top. She was pretty sure she should only ask for a very tiny miracle. Her eyes rested on a small tree branch that must have blown down in the night. It was about 18 inches long, and it lay in the withered grass near the corner of the box hedge.

Sister Anna stood up. Then she sat down and closed her eyes.

I will use that stick, Lord. I'm going to lean it up against the back of this seat. If it's still there and still upright when I come back in the morning after prayers, it will be a sign that I should stop being the Sunday school teacher. If it's gone or has fallen down, it will be a sign that I should still be the Sunday school teacher.

Sister Anna opened her eyes and stood up again.

Her teeth began to chatter. She scuttled across the quiet garden, picked up the stick, and scuttled back again. The stick felt icy and brittle in her stiff fingers. She stood the stick upright, resting its tip on the ground behind the seat, and leaned the other end up against the back of the seat. The back of the seat was covered in tree bark because the seat had been carved from an old stump. The tip of her stick rested neatly between two ridges in the bark. It looked like it would probably still be standing in the morning.

Sister Anna glanced around the garden. For some reason, she felt nervous.

Well, I can't think of anything else to do, Lord, so this will be it. There's the stick. I will come back in the morning.

She started to walk away, then stopped and looked

back over her shoulder. The stick was still there, motion-less, leaning against the seat.

Lord, have mercy on me, a sinner.

Sister Anna ran out of the prayer garden.

CHAPTER

SIX

THE CHILDREN surged up the stairs from the classroom and poured out the door, struggling into their coats as they ran. Elias led the way, shouting for Sam.

"Sam! Where did you go? What's happening? Sam!"

Grace's legs were much shorter than Elias' legs, but she grabbed two big handfuls of skirt, one on each side, and ran as hard as she could to keep up. "Sam!" shouted Grace. "Sam, I want to see too!"

"Yippee!" cried Matthew, running in circles. "We

escaped from Sunday school!"

Elias turned and ran backwards, grinning at his brother. "Good thing Macrina's not here today!"

Matthew roared and beat his chest with both fists. Elias laughed.

"Look, there's Sam!" Grace swerved wildly, and now she was leading the way, with Elias and Matthew running behind her. The other children had forgotten what they came outside for and were starting a game of tag on the brown grass between the church and the nuns' quarters.

"The parents are going to catch them," panted Elias, looking back at his classmates.

"Too bad they didn't come out to help with the goats, like us," laughed Matthew.

In front of them, Grace suddenly stopped short. Elias and Matthew flung themselves sideways and crashed onto the grass, just missing her.

"What on earth is wrong with you, Grace?" Elias rolled over and sat up, rubbing his elbow.

"I just thought!" Grace's eyes shone. "This could be my story for the book!"

"Huh?" Matthew stared at her. "What book?"

"You know. *The* book. For the monastery celebration."

"Oh, I forgot about that," said Matthew. He stood up. "Look, they caught the goats already without us."

"What?" Elias leaped up. "No way!" He looked around. A few yards ahead of them, Sister Katherine and Sam were leading two frisky goats through the gate of the animal farm. Saucer was prancing behind them, nipping at the heels of the goats and racing around so quickly Elias couldn't believe that no one had stepped on him.

"Wow," said Elias. "We missed it."

"Doesn't matter," replied Matthew. "Either way, we got out of Sunday school."

"Yeah." Elias nodded, resting his hands on his hips. "But I wish we could have helped."

Grace was scrabbling through her coat pockets, paying no attention to either of them. "I had a paper in here. Where's my paper?"

"What paper?" asked Matthew.

"This paper!" Grace crowed triumphantly. She pulled a folded piece of paper out of her coat pocket. Two flat rocks and a broken pencil stub tumbled out with it.

On one side of the paper was a map she had been given to color in Sunday school. The other side was blank. "Now, I just need a pencil." She picked up the stub from the ground, saw that the point was broken, and began searching her pockets again.

"Would this work?" Elias fished a ballpoint pen out of his pocket. It had no lid, and one end of it had been chewed.

"Perfect!" beamed Grace. She sat down on the path, tucked her feet under her skirt, and smoothed the paper across her knee. "Quiet now, I need to concentrate when I write."

Matthew and Elias looked at each other.

"One day," muttered Grace, saying each word slowly so that she could write as fast as she was talking. "One day . . . . at . . . the . . . monastery . . ."

"That's going to take a while," said Matthew to Elias.

"Uh-huh."

Grace looked up. "It's okay. They always paint buildings forever. I have time. As long as I don't freeze solid sitting on this cold path."

"Good luck with that," said Elias. "Come on, Matthew. Let's go find out what everyone else is doing."

"Goats, goats, goats," whispered Grace to herself. "I wonder if I spelled 'monastery' the right way. It looks weird." She did not even notice that the boys had gone. Murmuring each word carefully, and drawing little pictures of the funny parts, Grace wrote the first part of her story, the part she had seen with her own eyes. Then she folded the paper and stuffed it, together with the pen, into her pocket. She stood up.

"Now I can go ask Sam about it. He can tell me what happened before I got out here!"

Grace skipped along the path, humming a little tune that went up and down but never quite turned into a song that anyone else would recognize. When she reached the gate to the animal farm, Sister Katherine was just coming out of it. Sam had stayed behind with Saucer, near the doghouse.

"Goodbye, Sam," said Sister Katherine, closing the gate. "You've got about an hour until the parents will be finished painting. Come inside if you feel too cold."

Sam nodded.

"Hi, Sam! Hi, Sister Katherine!" Grace ran the last few steps and climbed onto her favorite perch on the gate. "Did you get all your goats back?"

Sister Katherine smiled. "We did! Sam and Saucer rounded them up and brought them safely home."

"I'm writing a story about it for the book," announced Grace, clutching the top bar of the gate and dancing her feet around on the middle bar.

"That will be nice," said Sister Katherine.

"Elias might be writing a story. He hasn't decided. Macrina's writing a story, too," continued Grace, "and she thinks hers will be better than mine."

Sam frowned. "Macrina always thinks she's better than everyone."

"Let's try to keep a friendly spirit, you two." Sister Katherine smiled at them. "I'm sure you and Macrina will both write good stories, in your different ways."

"Yes, but only one gets to go in the book," Grace pointed out.

"Yes, but all the stories will be copied and shared with our guests at the celebration," Sister Katherine reminded her, "so I hope everyone in your class writes one! I'm off to help with the painting. I had to lay my brush right down and run when I saw those two goats escaping."

Sam sat down next to Saucer. "Bye, Sister Katherine."

"I'll see you later, Sam."

Grace watched Sister Katherine walk away. Then she turned back to Sam.

"Tell me the story, Sam!"

"What story?"

"Tell me what happened with the goats before we all came outside. I couldn't see much from inside the classroom." Grace hopped off the gate and sat down on the ground outside it. She peered at Sam through the bars for several seconds. "Oh, wait, I need to get my paper out." She pulled the folded paper and the chewed-up pen out of her pocket, unfolded the paper, and grasped the pen tightly. "Okay, now I'm ready."

Sam ducked his head. Saucer snuffed and laid his nose on Sam's leg.

"Tell me, Sam," urged Grace. "First, the goats got out. How did they get out? I want to write it down."

Sam's face turned red. He dug his fingers into Saucer's fur. Saucer lifted his head.

"Why don't you talk to me, Sam?" Grace pressed her face against the gate. "Tell me the story. Tell me what happened first, and then what came next, and then what happened last. The last part is easy. You got the goats back. I saw you!"

Sam pressed his chin against his chest. "Go away," he mumbled.

"What?"

"Go away. Just go away!"

"Why? Why can't you help me with the story?"

Sam stood up. "I don't want to talk to you." He turned his back and started down the little path between the pens in the animal farm. Saucer hopped up and followed him.

"Well, that isn't very nice," said Grace to herself. She sat still, looking at her paper and her pen. She wanted to finish the story, but she didn't have enough details. She could see Sam through the bars of the gate. It didn't look like he was coming back.

Grace sighed and stood up. She folded the paper and was about to stuff it back into her pocket when she had an idea. "Sister Katherine can tell me the story! She can tell me the story while she helps them paint."

Grace never waited to put her plans into action. She acted on them as soon as they entered her head. Grace charged off down the path, looking for Sister Katherine.

Inside the animal farm, Sam kept going until he reached the duck pen, which was the last pen at the back of the enclosure. Glancing over his shoulder, he saw Grace's sparkly hair beads waving in the breeze as she ran off down the path. He drew a deep breath, relieved. She was gone. Sam didn't know Grace very well yet, and he hated trying to talk when someone was staring right at him and asking him questions too fast, one right after another.

Sam leaned against the fence post beside the duck pond. It was a small pond. The nuns had made it two years ago when the ducks came to live at the monastery. They dug it out themselves, lined it with sand and pebbles, and planted long grass and rushes around the edge. The ducks loved it. Today, they were all tucked up in the long brown grass beside the pond. It was too cold to swim, even for a duck.

Sam knew the ducks by name. He liked to say their names out loud when he was alone. They sounded good. "Dickens, Shakespeare, Charlotte, Emily, Cuthbert, Ignatius, Katherine, Photios, Moses, and Daniel."

Saucer sat down on Sam's foot.

Sam said the names again. "Dickens, Shakespeare, Charlotte, Emily, Cuthbert, Ignatius, Katherine, Photios, Moses, and Daniel." He always said the names in the same order, going from the largest duck to the smallest.

Sam noticed that the ducks were huddled together. "I bet Sister Katherine puts you in the barn at night now," he said.

Sam's eyes found the long, low building beyond the little farm. It stood between the back fence and the woods, a few yards away from the building that housed the nuns and their guests. Sam was quiet for several minutes, standing still and thinking about that barn. Then he dropped down on one knee suddenly and put his hand on Saucer's head.

"Saucer, where do the animals go in winter?"

Saucer's ears perked up at the sound of his name. He wagged his stumpy tail.

"Where do the animals go to be warm at night?" asked Sam.

Saucer barked.

"Where?" asked Sam. "Show me."

Saucer barked and ran in a little circle.

"I wish you could answer. I wish you knew all my words, not just the easy ones."

He looked at the barn again.

"Saucer."

Saucer came close to Sam, almost nose to nose.

"Remember that time Elias said you could talk at midnight on Christmas Eve?"

Saucer's bright eyes were fixed on Sam's face. He seemed to hear every word.

"I'm going to find out. I'm going to come in the barn at midnight on Christmas Eve."

Saucer raised his front paw and rested it on Sam's bent knee.

"I'm not going to tell anyone," said Sam, beginning to rub the furry spot between Saucer's ears. "People would just ruin it. I'm going to come by myself. You'll be there, Saucer. You and all the animals."

Saucer pressed his head into Sam's palm. He loved having his head rubbed.

"I'll stay awake all night. And then I'll know if it's true." Sam stood up.

Saucer sat back on his haunches, looking up at Sam with his bright black eyes.

Sam looked down at Saucer's trustful face.

"I hope it's true," said Sam.

WHEN SISTER ANNA WOKE UP in the morning, she
was too embarrassed to go and see if the stick was still
standing up against the back of her seat in the prayer garden. At first, she felt very silly for setting up a stick and
asking God for a sign. But then she felt that since she *had*
set up the stick, and told God about it, the least she could
do was to go and see whether it fell over.

But what if it did? Would it actually mean
anything?

Sister Anna wasn't sure.

What if it *did* mean something and she *didn't* go and see it?

Sister Anna thought and thought, and every few minutes, she changed her mind.

This went on all day until Vespers. As she stood in church, chanting the evening prayers, she made up her mind.

Enough of this nonsense, she said to herself. *I started this, and I'm going to finish it. As soon as Vespers is over, I'm going out to check on the stick.*

By that time, it was dark outside. The monastery was several miles outside the town, surrounded on three sides by woods. It would be very dark in the prayer garden.

Sister Anna hurried back to her quarters and took a small flashlight from her drawer. She was so flustered she forgot to put on her coat, and the cold air soaked through her habit like water as she scurried along the path.

When she reached the prayer garden, she was completely out of breath. She stopped at the edge of the garden, panting. She pressed one hand against her chest and felt her heart beating hard. Sister Anna was nervous.

She peered into the blank darkness in front of her. The sky had been cloudy all day. There was no moonlight. Remembering the flashlight, she switched it on. A thin strand of light fell into the darkness like a fishing line falling into a lake. The light wavered around as Sister Anna tried to get her bearings. The light caught a strip of box hedge, some crumpled grass, and at last fell on the seat carved out of a tree stump, where Sister Anna had left her stick. She couldn't see the stick from here. It was behind the seat on the other side of the garden.

Sister Anna clutched her flashlight tightly. The

cold metal hurt her hands, but she didn't loosen her grip. She swallowed, once and then again. Then she started walking across the garden toward the tree stump.

Thump, thump. Sister Anna could hardly tell if the sounds she heard were her footsteps or her heartbeat. The two sounds seemed to blur together and pound inside her head.

Sister Anna was getting close to the stump. Three more steps, two more. Would the stick be there? Would it be standing up or lying on the ground?

"Sister Anna, what are you doing?"

The flashlight made a wide, wobbling arc as it flipped into the air. Sister Anna screamed and clutched her ears with fright.

"Why do you fear me?" The quiet voice came from

behind her, and Sister Anna recognized it.

"Oh, Gerontissa, you scared me so much! I didn't know you were here! It's dark. I couldn't see you."

"It is too small, this little light you brought." The abbess leaned on her walking stick and slowly reached down to pick the flashlight up from the ground where it had fallen.

Sister Anna's knees shook. She squeezed her hands tightly together.

"Here." Gerontissa came closer, holding out the flashlight. The tiny beam pointed upward, and Sister Anna could see the abbess's face.

Gerontissa was very old. Her face was like a map, full of lines and wrinkles, but her dark eyes were full of life. Her voice creaked, and she leaned on a gnarled wooden stick to walk anywhere she could not reach with a few steps. English was not the first language she had learned, and she did not use it in her private prayers.

"You are in the garden in the dark," said Gerontissa, still holding out the flashlight.

Sister Anna could not think of a single word to say.

"You are doing something here?"

"I came to look at a stick," blurted Sister Anna in a squeaky voice.

The abbess's eyebrows rose. "You look at a stick? In dark of night?"

"I set the stick up yesterday, and then I came to see if it fell down." Sister Anna clasped her hands and reclasped them, squeeze, squeeze. "If it fell down, or if it didn't."

Gerontissa frowned. "How does a stick matter, if it stand or fall?"

Sister Anna hung her head.

The abbess smiled, but Sister Anna did not see her smile. "You have made a test with your stick."

"Yes, Gerontissa."

"You set a trap for God. In the garden. With a stick."

Sister Anna looked up. "A trap for God? Oh, no, I wouldn't try to—how could I—how could it be a trap for God?"

"You want Him to tell you something now, and He has not told something for you to hear, so you set a trap for Him, to make Him tell." Gerontissa thrust the flashlight at Sister Anna. "Here, take this little light. You come with me."

Sister Anna caught the flashlight as it dropped from Gerontissa's hand. The abbess turned and started walking, leaning on her stick. Sister Anna started to follow her, then stopped, looking over her shoulder. She swung the beam of the flashlight toward the tree stump seat.

"No, you come now. Do not go back to look at the stick."

"I'm sorry, Gerontissa." Sister Anna turned the flashlight forward, trying to light the abbess's way as she walked.

"You are not sorry to me. It is God you have set your trap for."

Sister Anna trudged along behind the abbess, out of the garden, along the path, to the door of the church. A shaded light hung over the church door. Here, they could see each other in the soft glow.

Gerontissa rested one hand against the church door and leaned on her stick. "I think I know for what reason you have set up your stick."

Sister Anna felt surprised. "You do?"

"I have heard about the goats," explained her companion. "And also about the children who run out of your class."

They were silent for several moments, huddled under the light by the church door. Sister Anna's teeth were chattering. She tried biting her tongue to make them stop, but it was no good. She was too cold.

"Gerontissa, I'm a bad teacher. Only Macrina listens to me, and she only listens so she can tell the other children what I said."

Gerontissa chuckled. "That one thinks she will be a nun, when she is grown."

"You don't think so?"

The abbess made a sound that might, or might not, have been a snort. Suddenly, she let go of the church wall and reached out her hand to Sister Anna. Sister Anna held it with her stiff, numb fingers.

"You are too cold," said Gerontissa, smiling. "So I will talk short. You gave up, little one. You make your trap because you think you are bad teacher, and someone else will be better. Macrina even, or Sister Katherine. Is it true?"

Sister Anna gasped. "Yes!"

"Why you think I make you teacher, hmm? I could ask Sister Katherine, but I don't ask her. Why you think?"

"I d-don't know, Gerontissa."

"Because Sister Katherine is all grown up. She is good and kind. But she does not remember so well as you do what it was like, when she was younger."

"But they don't listen to me! They would listen to Sister Katherine. She can lead them."

"You can lead them, if you stop trying to be Sister Katherine!" Gerontissa squeezed Sister Anna's hand. "Go inside and talk to God in His house. In there, it is warm."

Sister Anna grasped the carved wooden cross that served as a door handle. A breath of warm, scented air washed over her as she began to open the door.

"Sister Anna!" The abbess had stopped a few feet down the path.

"Yes?"

"You come to me, next time. Before you make traps with a stick."

Sister Anna crossed herself and slipped into the church. The air was warm, steeped with scents of incense and beeswax. Sister Anna tiptoed across the quiet space till she reached the iconostasis. Her face and hands, numbed by cold, began to tingle with returning life. Sister Anna knelt down and rested her forehead on the clean wooden floor.

Lord Jesus Christ, Son of God, have mercy on me, a sinner. Lord Jesus, I am so very sorry about the stick.

CHAPTER

EIGHT

MACRINA HAD MISSED CHURCH for two weeks. It was because of bronchitis. Grace knew this because she lived next door to Macrina, and Macrina's mother had told Grace's mother that Macrina had bronchitis. Grace had asked her mother what bronchitis was, because she'd never heard of it and it sounded important. Sort of like a dinosaur, but apparently not as much fun.

"It's like a very, very bad cold," said Grace's mother. "Macrina had a fever and a big cough, and she lost her voice completely for days!"

"She lost her voice?"

Grace's mama nodded. "Yes, she did. She couldn't talk at all, poor lamb."

Grace stared at her mother. She couldn't even *imagine* Macrina without a voice. It seemed like Macrina would have evaporated into thin air if she couldn't talk.

"Maybe you could make her a 'get well' card," suggested Grace's mother.

So Grace got out her colored pencils and drew a picture of Macrina talking on one side of the paper, and wrote, "I bet you can't wait to talk again" on the other side of the paper. She stared at the paper for a few minutes. There was still room to write more, and Grace's mother would probably tell her to write more. Grace's mother always liked Grace to be thorough.

Grace had written her first sentence in green, but she decided this next bit of writing should be in bright magenta.

"You can't believe what happened at Sunday school while you were gone. Get well soon, Grace."

These two sentences took Grace several minutes to write. She liked writing, but she liked to mumble the words to herself as she wrote and take time to make each letter fancy.

Grace held up the paper. It was now full. She slid off her bed, where she had been sitting with her art box and a clipboard, and went downstairs to show the card to her mother.

"That's nice, dear, but you didn't tell her what happened."

"It's okay," said Grace. "It will help her be interested to come back."

Grace's mother laughed.

Sure enough, Macrina was back at church three days later. Probably it was because she was better, but Grace liked to think that her card had something to do with it.

When the service ended, the families walked across to the refectory for lunch before their afternoon of work at the monastery. Grace searched through the crowd until she found Macrina walking along behind her parents. Even for the short walk from church to lunch, Macrina was bundled up in her coat, with a hat on under the hood, a woolly scarf, and gloves.

"Hi, Macrina!"

Macrina turned sideways to see who was talking to her. She was so bundled up that she couldn't turn her head. "Hello, Grace." She reached up to pull the scarf down from over her mouth. "Thank you for the nice card. My mom gave it to me."

Grace smiled happily. "You're welcome!"

They walked a few steps more and had almost reached the refectory door when Macrina spoke again. "Do you want to sit with me at lunch?"

"Sure!" Grace gave a little skip. She was now even more certain that her card had brought Macrina back to health. Why else would Macrina want to sit with her? Grace scurried off to pick up her lunch and prepared to enjoy a lengthy retelling of the goat escapade. She knew the whole story now. She had interviewed Sister Katherine about it last Sunday, and when she got home from church, she spent an hour carefully writing it down.

Of course, she didn't plan to tell Macrina that this was her story for the celebration book. Macrina had never told Grace what story she was writing, so Grace wasn't going to tell Macrina either. She was just going to tell

Macrina what she missed by being sick because it was too good a story to keep to herself, and she was positive Macrina would be interested. Macrina would be stunned!

Grace sat down at the long table at the end of the refectory where the children always gathered to eat their lunch together. Conversations at the children's table were always more interesting than those at the grown-up tables, at least in the opinion of the children.

Grace saw Macrina approaching. She scooted herself in from the end of the bench, making room. Macrina placed her tray neatly on the table and seated herself daintily on the end of the bench.

Grace started her story as soon as prayers were over.

"You know what happened while you were gone?"

Macrina fixed her eyes on Grace's face. "In your

card, you said something happened in Sunday school." She picked up her fork and took a bite of rice without moving her eyes.

Grace took a large gulp of juice and set her cup down with a bang. "The goats got out, and everyone in the whole class ran away!"

"What?!" Macrina dropped her fork. It clattered onto the floor, and she had to go get a clean one. Macrina never ran indoors, but Grace noticed she walked very quickly back to the table, clutching the new fork tightly in her hand. Macrina whisked into her seat.

"Two goats," said Grace. "But we didn't know that at first. Saucer got up and ran away from the window all of a sudden, and Sam went out to see why Saucer left."

Macrina nodded, chewing quickly and politely with her mouth closed.

"So then," continued Grace, "we all got chairs to stand on and smashed our faces against the window so we could see where Sam and Saucer went. At least, Elias and the taller kids smashed their faces," she amended. "I couldn't reach, so I had to keep asking what they could see."

"But—but—" spluttered Macrina.

"So then Elias saw Saucer herding goats, and it was two goats who escaped out of the goat pen! Saucer was running around biting at their legs to make them go back home, and it was awesome! All the kids just jumped right off the chairs and ran outside to see."

Macrina almost choked on her food. "They ran after goats? Right in the middle of class? What about Sister Anna?"

Grace paused. She couldn't remember anything

about Sister Anna at all. "I don't know. She was there. I mean, she's always there, isn't she? But we were all excited about the goats, so we just ran!"

Macrina opened and shut her mouth several times. It looked like she had so many things to say that she couldn't decide what to say first.

Grace was pleased. This was the first time she had talked to Macrina that Macrina had actually been interested in what she had to say. Grace's mother was always pointing out how nice it would be for the girls to be friends, since they lived next door to each other and were only a year apart in age, but up until now, Grace had been doubtful that it would work.

"But what happened?" asked Macrina. "Did you go back to class?"

"No, we went to see the goats. And don't worry!

Saucer chased them all the way back to their pen. I saw Sister Katherine putting them back in and shutting the gate."

"Yes, but didn't you all get in trouble?"

Grace shook her head. "No, we didn't." Now that she thought about it, Grace realized that was surprising.

"Didn't the parents know?" asked Macrina incredulously. "The whole class ran outside chasing goats, and nobody *noticed*?"

"We didn't actually chase the goats," Grace pointed out. "We just watched Saucer chase them. At least, some of us did. Some of the kids just went to play tag, I think."

"Tag?!?" Macrina set down her fork so it wouldn't go flying and turned herself in her seat so she could look at Grace full on. "That's so mean! How do you think Sister Anna felt when everyone ran away from her class? I can't believe none of you got in trouble. The parents didn't know. That's the only explanation. Sister Anna was too nice to tell them."

Grace stared at Macrina, round-eyed. This was a side of the event she had not thought about at all. Maybe she should re-write her story for the monastery book. How could they print a story where a nun's feelings got hurt and nobody noticed?

"I didn't think of that," said Grace. "Sister Anna didn't say anything to us the next week. She just let us sit on the rug, and she told us the Bible story and let us color a picture."

Macrina slid off the bench and picked up her tray. "I'm going to find Sister Anna right now. If I had known all that, I would have talked to her at class today."

Grace felt uneasy. "Do you think she wants you to talk to her?"

Macrina paused. "What do you mean?"

"You weren't there," said Grace, struggling to put her uneasy feeling into words. "You didn't run after the goats."

"Of course I didn't! If I had been there, I would have stayed in class and helped her keep the other kids from running."

"But if you say that, she will know people are talking about when we ran way," said Grace.

"What's the matter? Are you afraid you're going to get in trouble?" asked Macrina.

"You said we should think of Sister Anna's feelings," said Grace, in a small voice.

"So?"

"So, do you think it will hurt her feelings that you found out what happened?"

"Oh." Macrina set her tray down again and stood still, frowning, tapping her fingers on the edge of the table.

"Are you going to tell?" asked Grace, after a moment.

"I should," said Macrina huffily. She picked up her tray. "But I need to think about it."

Grace watched Macrina walk over to the counter where dirty dishes were placed. Macrina set her tray down and sorted her dishes into the bins—silverware in one bin, cups in another, plates and other dishes in the last. Suddenly, Macrina whirled around and came quickly back to Grace.

"They must know already," said Macrina, dropping down onto the end of the bench. "Sister Katherine saw you, and Sister Anna probably told Gerontissa."

Grace looked doubtful. "I guess so."

"And still none of you got in trouble! Nobody said anything."

"Nope!"

"That doesn't make any sense."

Grace thought for a minute. "The nuns are nice. Maybe they didn't mind that we went outside. Maybe they could understand."

Macrina shook her head. "It's not about being nice.

What would happen if everyone just ran out of Sunday school whenever they felt like it?"

Grace had no idea.

Macrina stood up, still shaking her head. "It's not right. It shouldn't have happened."

Grace looked up at Macrina's disapproving face. Somehow, this was not how she had imagined the conversation going.

"I'm going to find my parents," said Macrina. She walked away.

Grace leaned her chin on her hand. She sighed.

"What was that all about?" asked Elias, scooting down the bench and coming to a stop beside Grace.

"I told Macrina about running after the goats,"

said Grace, with another long sigh.

"What did you do that for?" Elias snickered. "I bet she flipped out!"

"I thought she would talk to me if I said something interesting."

"Aw, don't worry about her, Gracie. Be friends with the people who like you for yourself!" Elias grinned at her, then jumped up. "Come on! I heard the parents are doing a job we actually get to help with today."

"Really?" Grace leaped out of her seat. "Is it paint? Wait for me, Elias! I can help!"

"I don't think it's paint, but you can help do whatever it is."

Elias waited while Grace took her tray to the dirty dishes counter, then together they ran outside. The families had gathered outside, and Sister Katherine was there. As Elias and Grace joined the group, Sister Katherine led the way down the path toward the building that housed the nuns' quarters and the guest house.

"What are we doing?" asked Elias, tapping the arm of a nearby mom.

"We're making beds and laying out towels in the guest rooms so they'll be ready for all the families to stay here next week on Christmas Eve!" she said, smiling kindly at Elias and Grace.

"Christmas Eve!" shouted Grace joyfully.

"Are you coming?" asked Elias. "We are."

"Of course we're coming!" Grace hopped and skipped. She stopped and caught Elias's arm. "Elias, I wonder if Sam will come."

"He's coming," said Elias. "He's coming with his parents. My mom told me."

"Do you think he will go in the barn?" asked Grace, lowering her voice.

"Go in the barn? What for?"

"For the animals. You remember, like you told him."

"Ohhhh. You mean to hear the animals talk at midnight on Christmas Eve?"

Grace nodded vigorously.

"I don't know. Won't he be asleep?"

"Maybe he could stay awake. Maybe I could stay awake. I want to go, too."

Elias shrugged. "I don't think your parents are

going to let you go in the barn in the middle of the night."

Grace thought that was probably true. "Maybe when I'm older," she said.

"If you still want to do it when you're older."

"Why wouldn't I want to do it when I'm older?" asked Grace.

"Maybe you will," said Elias. "It just seems like when people get older, they stop trying to find out about stuff anymore. Grown-ups just go to bed at night. They finally get old enough to boss their own life, and what do they do? They just go to bed."

"Every night?"

Elias nodded. "As far as I can see."

Grace frowned. "But if they all go to bed every

night, how do we know the animals talk at midnight on Christmas Eve?"

Elias shoved his hands into pockets and hunched up his shoulders.

"I guess we don't," he said sadly.

CHAPTER

NINE

IT WAS CHRISTMAS EVE. The church was full of nuns and families. The air was full of their voices, singing and praying. In the candlelight, the icons seemed to glow and flicker, as if they too were moving and breathing. Sam had to close his eyes every few minutes. But he kept opening them again. It was warm inside the church, and it smelled good. Best of all, Saucer was with him. Together they stood on a little red rug at the back of the church, put there especially for them by Sister Katherine.

Sam could see his dad and mom a few feet away, standing beside Aunt Eva and Uncle Rick. He could see

Elias and Matthew and their parents, and Grace and her parents. He could even see Macrina, if he wanted to. He could see Sister Anna and Sister Katherine and all the nuns. And Gerontissa. She was very small and very old, but Sam could see her standing, leaning on her stick.

Sam closed his eyes. He felt Saucer's nose, bumping against his leg. Sam opened his eyes and looked down at Saucer. Saucer looked up at Sam and laid a friendly paw on his foot.

Tonight, thought Sam. *Tonight, I'm going to hear you talk. You and the goats and the rabbits and everything. If you do talk. I hope you talk.*

Sam had a plan. After church, the families would all go to sleep in the guest rooms. The guest rooms were in the same building as the nuns' quarters, but they were on the first floor. The nuns lived upstairs, where visitors did not go.

It was a small monastery, and the animal farm was only a short walk along the path from the living quarters. Sam knew every inch of the monastery. He had explored it all this summer, with Saucer at his heels.

Sam looked down at Saucer again. *When everyone goes to sleep, that's when I'll go to the barn. I can watch the red numbers on the travel clock. Mom always brings the travel clock. We're going to bed early tonight, so we can get up early in the morning. They'll fall asleep before midnight. Then I'll go to the barn.*

Sam stopped thinking for a few minutes. He watched the candles and stared hard at an icon, trying to catch the saint actually moving. Did he move? Maybe not. It was the light moving. That's what made him seem alive.

When it was time, Sam walked up to take communion, and Saucer waited peacefully on the little red rug.

Together they listened to the end of the service. Together they slipped out the back door of the church. When he took Saucer back to his dog house and patted him to say goodnight, Sam noticed that Saucer's fur smelled like incense.

Sam's plan worked. His family went to bed not long after the service ended. His mother set the travel clock on the table by the bed. Sam could see the red numbers from his sleeping bag on the floor. He laid his coat next to him, and amazingly, his mother didn't tidy it away before she went to bed.

Sam's dad fell asleep first. Sam could hear the change in his breathing. But still he waited. It was only ten o'clock. He had to be sure his mother was asleep too before he got up.

At 10:20, Sam pushed back the top of his sleeping

bag and carefully sat up. It was a test. If his mother
was still awake, she would notice and ask if he needed
something.

Sam counted to five in his head, and then started
crawling out of his sleeping bag.

Nothing happened.

He lifted his coat with one hand and stood up.

Nothing happened.

Sam tiptoed to the door. His shoes were there. He
picked them up and tucked them under his arm with the coat.

Now all he had to do was get out the door.

Sam breathed in, then out, then in, then out. He
wrapped his hand around the doorknob and turned it,
very, very slowly.

Behind him, his father stirred. His arm twitched, and Sam's mother sighed in her sleep.

Sam froze. He rolled his eyes sideways so he could see the numbers on the travel clock again. He waited until a minute had passed. It was hard to hold the door knob twisted for sixty seconds, but Sam did it.

When a minute had passed, Sam pulled gently on the knob, and the door swung open. Like everything at the monastery, the door had been well cared for. It sat snugly on its hinges, and its hinges were well oiled. It did not make a sound when Sam opened it.

Sam tiptoed through the door. He blinked. The lights were on in the hall. He pulled the door shut behind him, trying to be slow and fast at the same time. He didn't want the light to wake up his parents, but he didn't want to bang the door.

With the door safely closed behind him, Sam set his shoes quietly on the floor and pushed his feet into them. He pulled on his coat, but decided to wait until he was outside to zip it up. Zippers made a zipper noise. It wasn't a big noise, but Sam wasn't taking any chances.

The door at the end of the hall was locked at night, but it could still be opened from the inside. Sam put both hands on the crossbar and pushed. The door swung slowly open. Sam held the crossbar with one hand and stepped outside. He grasped the handle on the outside of the door, let go of the inside of the door, and slowly, slowly let the door swing shut.

Phew!

He was out.

A small shaded bulb above the door made a pool of light around him. He went down two steps to the path, and hopped off the path onto the frosty grass.

Once away from the building, Sam tipped back his head and gulped the cold, clear air like a drink of water. Above him, Sam saw thousands of stars.

Stars are funny, thought Sam. *They make light we can see a billion million miles away, but they don't make enough light for me to see where I'm going in the dark.*

Sam ran lightly over the grass. He didn't need starlight to show him the way. Sam loved the barn. He could have found his way there with his eyes closed.

When he reached the barn, Sam ran his hand along the wall until he felt the doorframe, and then the handle. The barn had a sliding wooden door. Sam set his shoulder against the door, grabbed the handle, and pushed. It was a heavy door. He had helped Sister Katherine open it before, and it was hard to open it alone, but he pushed with all his strength. The door opened just a few inches. Sam pushed again, then turned sideways and wriggled through the opening. With a grunt, he pulled the door shut behind him.

Inside, the barn was as dark as a cave. Sam could smell the good farm smell of animals and hay. The air felt surprisingly warm, and Sam could hear the soft noises of the animals, wakened from sleep by the sound of his coming into the barn.

"Hello," said Sam to the darkness. "It's me."

Sam heard a rustling, scampering noise, and the next minute, Saucer was bounding around on the floor in front of him. He didn't bark, but he yipped and squeaked and pawed Sam's legs.

"Hey, buddy." Sam got down on his knees, and Saucer bounced up and put his paws on Sam's shoulders.

Sam rubbed his ears, and Saucer licked Sam's face.

"Come on, Saucer." Sam stood up and felt his way to the center of the barn. There were a few bales of hay piled there. Sam sat down on one of them and pulled Saucer up next to him.

His eyes had grown used to the darkness now. His eyes worked together with his ears and his nose, showing him the animals in their pens around him in the barn. He was pretty sure the goats were all standing in a row along the front of their pen, staring at him. Beside them, Bethlehem the donkey was peering at Sam over the door of his stall, nickering softly.

The bunnies were in a hutch on the other side of the hay bales, and Sam could hear the thump of their soft feet as they hopped back to bed. He couldn't see the ducks, but he knew they liked to nest in the goat pen.

Sam felt around in the dark behind him and discovered there were two bales of hay stacked up behind the one he was sitting on. He scooted back and leaned against the bale behind him. Saucer curled up beside Sam and rested his head on Sam's leg. Sam laid his hand on Saucer's head.

A curious feeling of contentment came to Sam. He was warm. He was proud that his plan to come to the barn had worked. He was glad that Saucer was there with him, waiting for midnight to come.

Ever since Elias had told him about the animals talking on Christmas Eve, Sam had felt worried. He worried that the animals wouldn't really talk. He worried that they would talk, but he wouldn't be able to get to the barn to hear them. He worried that Grace would remember the story too and try to come with him. He worried that the animals wouldn't talk because he was there to hear them.

He worried that the story might not even be true. He wasn't sure why it mattered so much, but it did.

Sam sighed. He was here. Saucer was here. Now all he had to do was wait.

It would be a long wait. The clock had said 10:23 just before he left the room. Sam wasn't sure how long he had been in the barn, but he figured he had at least another hour to go till midnight.

Around him, the animals moved and breathed and settled down. Like the church full of people, the barn with its animals felt full of life. Sam liked that feeling of fullness, but it could be a little overwhelming. Sam closed his eyes to take a break.

His eyes popped open. What if he fell asleep?

Sam opened his eyes as wide as he could. Saucer stirred and licked Sam's knee.

Sam rubbed the furry space between Saucer's ears. Saucer's fur was warm and soft. Sam's hand relaxed.

A piece of hay tickled Sam's ear. Sam moved his head to a more comfortable spot.

Saucer went to sleep. Sam could hear his breathing slow. Sam rubbed his neck. Saucer's ears twitched, and he lifted his head.

"Don't fall asleep, Saucer. You have to talk to me at midnight."

Saucer snuffed at Sam and lay down again.

Sam stared into the darkness. It was a funny feeling, staring hard and seeing almost nothing. Sam chose the darkest corner of the barn and stared at it as hard as he could. Nothing. Blackness. He closed his eyes and opened them. Nothing.

If I was blind, thought Sam, *it would feel like this. I would stare at stuff, but see nothing.*

Sam felt sleepy. He wondered how much longer he had to wait.

Saucer's leg twitched.

I bet he's dreaming. Dog dreams. What do dogs dream about? I don't know. I'm not a dog.

Sam sighed. *That's why I want to hear him talk. So I can know what he thinks. It's like the dark. I can't see in the dark, and I can't see in Saucer's brain.*

Saucer was warm. He was keeping Sam warm, resting against him on the bale of hay.

Sam's eyes closed. He knew he was falling asleep, but he couldn't stop it. For a few seconds, he thought he was waking himself up again. Then he gave up.

It's okay. They'll wake me up when they start talking.

Sam slept.

CHAPTER

TEN

GRACE'S VOICE woke Sam in the morning.

"I know where he is! He's in here!"

There was a scuffling sound, as Grace tried and failed to open the barn door by herself.

Sam opened his eyes. He saw wooden rafters and then, abruptly, a goat's face hovering above him.

Sam stared at the goat, and the goat stared at Sam. Sam decided he must be dreaming and closed his eyes again.

A warm, wet doggy tongue began licking Sam's face.

"Uff," grunted Sam, turning his head from side to side to escape the wet tongue. He rolled over, wiping his face. He opened his eyes again.

Sam had gone to sleep sitting on a hay bale, but he woke up on the floor of the barn with the hay bale directly behind him. In front of him, in a semi-circle, sat every animal in the barn. The goats, the ducks, the bunnies, Aero the dog and his best friend Butterscotch the chicken, even Bethlehem the donkey had come out of his pen. Some were awake, like Bethlehem and the inquisitive goat, and some were still dozing. They were cuddled together side by side, keeping Sam and each other warm on the floor of the barn.

Before Sam could take it all in, the barn door slid

open and Grace sprang through it, with Sister Anna and Sister Katherine right behind her.

"Here he is!" cried Grace triumphantly.

Sam scrambled to his feet and backed against the hay bale. The animals started milling around, bleating and squawking, telling the two nuns about the midnight visitor in the barn.

"Hello, Sam," said Sister Katherine. "Are you all right?"

Sam shook his head back and forth, like a swimmer trying to clear water from his ears.

"Are you cold?" asked Sister Anna. She held out a blanket.

Sam's parents appeared in the doorway.

"Sammy, what happened?" cried his mother, pushing past the nuns and trying to put her arms around her son.

"He came to hear the animals," said Grace helpfully.

"No!" shouted Sam, breaking away from his mom. "They don't talk, Grace! I was here all night! They don't talk!"

Sam put his head down and plowed through the space between Sister Katherine and Sister Anna. Saucer lunged to his feet and stampeded through the animals, following Sam.

Sam ran past his father in the doorway. Grace started to follow him, but Sam's mother caught her arm.

"Let him have a minute, honey," she said.

The four grown-ups stood still, looking at each other. The animals began to drift away, going back to their pens, nipping the hay, talking among themselves.

"I could help," said Sister Anna suddenly. She turned to Sam's mother and father. "Will you let me go talk to him?"

"He can be pretty tough when he's upset," said Sam's father. "Sometimes he needs to be by himself to calm down."

"How can you help?" asked Sam's mother.

"I just thought maybe I know why he was here," said Sister Anna, shifting the blanket from one arm to the other.

"He was here because Elias told him the animals could talk at midnight on Christmas Eve," explained

Grace, looking around the circle of grown-up faces. "I bet he wanted to hear Saucer talk."

"Poor Sammy," said his mother. There were tears in her eyes.

The church bell began to ring.

"Better go find your parents, Grace," said Sam's father.

Grace didn't want to leave the barn. She wanted to know how the conversation ended. But Sam's father was holding the door open for her. Grace ran through it, back down the path to find her parents and go to church.

Grace went to the Christmas morning liturgy with her family. The church was full of families, praying and singing joyfully. But Grace did not feel joyful. She kept thinking about Sam. Looking around the church, she knew that most people had no idea Sam had spent the night in the barn and had run out of it crying in the morning. She could see Sister Katherine up front. Sister Katherine knew. She couldn't see Sam's parents. She turned her head and saw the little red rug in the back of the church, where Sam had stood with Saucer last night. It was empty.

Grace decided to pray. She was in church, after all. It seemed like the thing to do.

Why didn't the animals talk to him, Lord Jesus? Maybe they talked and he fell asleep and didn't hear. Why didn't You wake him up?

When the liturgy ended, Grace followed her parents out of the church. She saw Elias and ran ahead to catch up with him.

"Hi, Grace. Merry Christmas," said Elias.

Grace caught his arm and stood on tiptoes to reach his ear. "Elias, Sam went to the barn last night, and the animals didn't talk."

Elias stopped walking. "They didn't? What happened?"

"I don't know, but when his parents woke up this morning, he wasn't in the room. We were in the room next door, so we came out to help them look. I remembered about the animals and Christmas Eve, and that's where we found him."

"Wow."

People streamed around them, making their way to the Christmas feast laid out in the refectory.

"How do you know the animals didn't talk?" asked Elias.

"Sam yelled it to me when we found him."

"I didn't see him at church."

"Me neither. I don't know where he is."

"That's sad."

They started walking again.

"Elias?"

"What?"

"Why didn't the animals talk to Sam?"

"I don't know, Gracie." Elias sighed. "Maybe he didn't hear them. Or maybe they don't really talk."

CHAPTER

ELEVEN

IT WAS JANUARY 6, the Feast of Theophany and the day on which the children would be reading their stories in Sunday school and voting on which would be included in the book for the monastery celebration.

Sister Anna met them at the door of the classroom and welcomed them in, one at a time.

"Find your seats quickly, children. We want to have time to hear all of your stories."

Everyone was excited and full of curiosity. What would the stories be about? Which story would win the contest to be in the book?

Sam came in after the other children were seated. He sat down and looked out the window. Outside, Saucer sat on his haunches, puffing hot doggy breath and fogging up the glass.

Sister Anna stood at the front of the classroom with her hands clasped, smiling at the children. Beside her was a wooden podium, which faced the class. "When it's your turn to read, you can stand up here in front. See? I brought this podium from upstairs for you to use while you're reading your story. Who would like to go first?"

Macrina's hand shot up.

"All right, Macrina. Come right up."

Macrina had typed her story on the computer, printed it out, and put it into a manila folder so the paper wouldn't get creased or dirty. When Sister Anna called on her, she stood up, pushed in her chair, and carried her folder up to the podium.

Elias leaned back in his chair and crossed his arms on his chest. Grace tucked one foot under her so that she could sit up higher and see better.

Macrina opened her folder, shuffled her papers, cleared her throat, and began to read.

The History of the Monastery of Saint Gerasim and the Lion

By Macrina Anne Smith

ONE DAY IN 1978, two nuns came to America to start a monastery. The nuns were sisters in real life, before they were nuns, and one of them was blind. When they would walk anywhere, the nun who could see would hold the other nun's hand so she didn't run into anything.

When they got to America, they visited the bishop of our state and asked for his blessing to start a monastery. He gave them his blessing, and a family who lives in our town gave them a little house at the edge of an old farm. The farmer had died, and there was no one to run the farm any more. There were a few animals left, and the barn was still standing. Most of the land was covered with woods. The nuns cleaned the house and the barn, and they started praying for a whole monastery to be built there.

Other nuns came to join them, and in three years, they had enough money to start building a church. They kept on working and more nuns kept on coming, and they finished the church building in 1983. The next year, the first two nuns got a letter. It was from their family back at home in their old country. Their mother's sister had died, and she had left all her money to the monastery. She had a lot of money. The nuns could finish building their whole monastery now, and they rejoiced.

Some people might want to know why the monastery is called the Monastery of Saint Gerasim and the Lion. Saint Gerasim was an abbot at a monastery in the Holy Land a long time ago. He is also called Saint Jerome. He helped a lion with a hurt paw, and the lion became his friend and lived at the monastery. The nuns chose this saint because they helped the animals who lived at the farm that used to be here, and the farm turned into a monastery, just like Saint Gerasim's lion sort of turned into a monk.

Macrina paused and looked around at her classmates and then at Sister Anna. Then she turned to the last page on the podium in front of her.

In closing, I can say that the nuns who live here now have animals too, and they care for their animals and for all the people who come to the monastery. A good example is Sister Anna, who cares about us and teaches us Sunday school.

The End

Macrina gave a little nod, almost like a bow, and smiled at Sister Anna. Sister Anna smiled back. Grace looked from one to the other. She thought it was nice that Macrina had mentioned Sister Anna. Maybe that's how she decided to make Sister Anna feel better, thought Grace to herself, remembering her conversation with Macrina before Christmas.

The children clapped politely, and Macrina returned to her seat.

"Who would like to go next?" asked Sister Anna.

Two more children raised their hands, and Sister Anna had them read their stories, one at a time. Grace listened to the first story, but then she got out her own story and re-read it while the second child was reading his story. She decided she was ready to raise her hand, so as soon as he sat down, she raised it.

"Go ahead, Grace," said Sister Anna.

Grace came to the front of the room and set her story carefully on the podium, but when she stood behind it, she couldn't see a thing.

"Here," said Elias, jumping up. "Use a chair." He seized an empty chair from the end of the table and pushed it around behind the podium.

"Thank you," said Grace, climbing up on the chair. Elias grinned at her and sat down.

"Ahem," said Grace. "This is my story." She stared at her classmates until they were quiet.

"One day, we were having Sunday school and Saucer was right outside the window," began Grace, reading more quickly than usual because she knew what all the words would be. "He always sits there, snuffing and puffing on the glass and watching Sam. But this day, he got up and ran off, and Sam went to see why."

Grace stopped for a moment. In the first version of the story, she had written about all the children running out of class to see the escaped goats, but this was her new version. She had taken that part out, so she wouldn't hurt Sister Anna's feelings. She kept reading.

> Sam and Saucer found two goats who
> had escaped from the animal farm and were

running around the monastery, making goat noises and eating stuff goats don't get to eat.

Several of her classmates giggled. Grace felt pleased.

But Saucer is a herding dog, so Sam told him to round up the goats. Sister Katherine came too, and when Saucer chased the goats back to their pen, Sister Katherine shut it tight behind them. Then Sister Katherine said sorry to the goats and sorry to Sam and Saucer. She said she must have left the gate open, and it was her fault the goats got out.

Sister Anna gasped.

Grace turned to her. "Did you ask something?"

Sister Anna blushed. "No, dear. I—I just jumped because your story was so interesting."

"That's good," said Grace. She picked up her paper and continued.

> This is a true story for the monastery book. I interviewed Sister Katherine to get it, and also, I saw Sam and Saucer chase the goats back with my own eyes. I picked this story to write about because I love how there is always something going on at the monastery. I never know what will happen when I come here, but all the things that happen have a happy ending.

Grace folded up her paper and jumped down from her chair. Her classmates clapped and giggled until she was all the way back in her seat. Grace smiled at all of them. She was pleased. Her story had turned out well. Even if it did not go in the book, she had enjoyed reading it to her friends.

Sister Anna came over to the podium. "Are there any other children who would like to read?"

Macrina glanced around at her classmates. Elias wiggled his eyebrows at her.

"Well, if that's all—" began Sister Anna.

"No," said Sam. "It's not all."

Everyone in the room turned with one motion and stared at Sam. Sam never talked in class. He had been completely silent while the other children read their stories. He sat in his chair, staring at Saucer waiting for him outside the window.

"Do you have a story to share?" asked Sister Anna.

Sam stood up and pulled a folded paper out of his back pocket.

"Come and read it," said Sister Anna, smiling and patting the podium.

Sam pushed back his chair with his foot and walked to the podium. The whole class watched his every move. Sam didn't look at them. He put his paper on the podium and carefully unfolded it. His fingers trembled a little. He smoothed out the paper and glanced at Saucer, whose nose was pressed against the glass.

Sam made a choking, gargling sound, clearing his throat. There was no other sound in the room. He lifted his paper, holding it with his fingertips, and began to read.

"Here is something to put in the monastery book." His voice sounded raspy and hoarse at first. "It is not a story. It is something that happened."

Sam stopped. The children heard a scrabbling, clicking sound as Saucer pawed the window. Sam continued.

On Christmas Eve at midnight, I was in
the barn. I heard a story that animals can talk
then, for one hour. It's the only time they talk
that people can hear them and know what
they say. I like animals, especially Saucer. So
I went.

Sam stopped again. He set his paper down carefully
and wiped his face on his sleeve. Then he picked up the
paper and started reading again.

I went to sleep in the barn, and I didn't
hear the animals talk. I woke up in the morning, and I ran away because I was too sad
to stay. I wanted to hear Saucer talk, really
bad. But I didn't hear him. Maybe he talked.
Maybe he didn't. I don't know if it's true or
if it's a fake that animals talk at midnight on
Christmas.
    That whole day, my parents tried to talk
to me and help me feel better. I know they

care about me, and that's good. But I felt sad
about Christmas Eve.

The next Sunday, Sister Anna came to
find me when I was by myself outside the
barn. She said one time, she had a day like I
did. It was a day when she tried to make God
tell her something when it wasn't the right
time. At first, I didn't know what she meant.
But she said, "Sam, you are like me. You set
a trap for God. You want to know something
God isn't ready to tell you, so you tried to
make Him tell you. But you have to wait, like
me."

Sam took a deep, ragged breath and flipped his

paper over. There was more writing on the back.

You might think that was just an excuse.
You might think Sister Anna was trying to
make God look good because the animals
talking was a fake. But wait, because there
was one more thing.

The children were leaning forward now. Grace looked at Elias. She knew he was wondering the same thing she was wondering. What was the one more thing?

Sister Anna said sometimes we are so busy pushing God to show us one thing that we don't see that He is showing us something else. I asked her what does that mean, and she said she saw something when they found me in the barn. What she saw was all the animals sitting with me. When I went to sleep, they were all in their own parts of the barn, in their pens. Only Saucer was with me. But when I woke up, they were sitting together in a circle around me. They kept me warm, and they stayed with me until I woke up.

Sam set the paper down one more time and wiped his face on his shirt sleeve. He took a big breath and picked up the paper.

When someone finds this book about the monastery a hundred years from now, I want them to know that I wish I had stopped to look at the animals who were there with me. I ran out of the barn. I was angry because I didn't hear them speak. I didn't stop and remember that Saucer and Aero can open pens. They get on their back legs and flip the catch up with their noses. On Christmas Eve, they opened pens for me, and the animals came out for me. And I didn't even notice. Next year, I'm going back. And when I wake up and the animals are all around me, I'm going to stay there with them and say thanks.

Sam drew a long, trembling breath. Sister Anna came toward him, and he handed her his paper. Outside the window, Saucer barked. Sam ducked around Sister Anna and ran out of the room.

The children sat still. Sister Anna stood in front of them, holding Sam's paper.

Suddenly, Grace stood up. She stood up so quickly that her chair fell over. Everyone jumped.

"I vote we put Sam's story in the book," said Grace loudly. "I liked writing my story, and I think Macrina liked writing her story. But Sam's story is the most important. That's the story that should go in the book."

"That's right," cried Elias. "I vote for Sam!"

"Me too," said Matthew, and the other children chimed in. "We vote for Sam! Put Sam's story in the book!"

The classroom was quite loud for a minute or two, and then everyone turned to Macrina, who had stayed quiet, meeting no one's eyes.

"Hush, now," said Sister Anna, setting Sam's story

carefully on the podium. "We'll raise our hands. That's the best way."

The children settled down.

"Raise your hand if you would like Sam's story to be chosen for the book," said Sister Anna.

Hands shot into the air all over the classroom. Every child voted for Sam. Everyone except Macrina.

Sister Anna looked at their eager faces and the hands waving high in the air. "Thank you, children," she said. She paused. "Macrina, is there anything you'd like to say before we make the final decision?"

Heads turned.

Macrina smoothed her tidy manila folder. Then she looked up. "Can we still share our stories at the celebration?" she asked wistfully.

Sister Anna smiled. "Of course, dear. I'm going to make copies of all your stories, and we'll hand them out to each guest who comes to the celebration. All of your stories were beautiful, in different ways. I don't want any of them to be lost."

Elias sat forward in his chair. "Macrina, I have an idea!"

Macrina turned in her seat. "What is it?"

"You could send your story to the newspaper. The one from our town. I bet they will have an article about the monastery when the celebration happens."

Macrina's eyes gleamed. She turned to Sister Anna. "How do you send a story to the newspaper?"

Sister Anna laughed. "I don't know how, Macrina, but I'm sure Sister Katherine can help you."

"I'll ask her after class," said Macrina.

Sister Anna looked around the classroom. "So we've decided. Sam is the one whose story will go in the book."

"I want to tell him!" said Grace excitedly.

"I want to tell him, too!" said Elias.

Sister Anna glanced at the window. Saucer's spot was empty. "Actually, I want to tell him myself," she said. "You children go upstairs and tell your families. Thank you all for your hard work and for being such good listeners when your friends were reading. Have a blessed feast day!"

"Happy Theophany!"

"Happy Theophany!"

The tide of children swelled and rolled out of the classroom, down the hall, and up the stairs. Sister Anna heard their joyful voices, bringing the good news.

Alone in the classroom, Sister Anna closed her eyes and bowed her head.

"Glory to God in the highest," she said.

EPILOGUE

Saucer sat by his doghouse, enjoying the warm spring evening. Every now and then he threw back his head, sniffing the flower-scented air and listening to the sounds of happy voices coming from the open windows of the refectory.

Saucer turned his head. He heard a scuffling sound, coming from the nearby gate of the animal farm. Saucer stood up.

"It's me," said Sam, climbing over the top of the fence and dropping down on the ground beside Saucer. "I didn't want to wake all the other animals up, squeaking the gate."

Saucer snuffed and puffed. He bounced from one paw to the other. He licked Sam's shoe.

"You should see that party in there," said Sam, sitting down beside Saucer. "That's the most people I ever saw at the monastery."

Saucer flopped down next to Sam. His front legs stuck out in front of him. His back legs stuck out in back of him.

"You look like Super Dog when you do that," said Sam. He rubbed the furry spot between Saucer's ears.

They sat together in the twilight.

"They put my story in the book," said Sam.

Saucer sat up.

"It's in there forever. If I have great-great-ten-times-great grandchildren, they could come here and read that book, and it would have a story in it by me."

Saucer barked and pawed Sam's leg. Sam put his arm around Saucer.

"I didn't ever think that would happen. I didn't even know I could ever write something like that."

Saucer licked Sam's ear.

"It's like trying to look at the dark," said Sam, remembering his night in the barn. "You can't make your eyes see something without any light."

Saucer cocked his head and looked puzzled.

"Knowing things before they happen," explained Sam. "You can't. Just like you can't see in the dark."

Saucer rested his head on Sam's shoulder. He

didn't say anything because even a corgi can't speak to a human with human words. But Sam didn't mind. He sat still, feeling Saucer's breath in his ear.

"I love you, Saucer," Sam said.

THE END

MELINDA JOHNSON is an Orthodox Christian, wife, mother, and writer. She loves words, and she loves the miraculous inner worlds we create with them. Melinda is the bemused and enchanted guardian of a corgi named Ferdinand. Ferdinand enjoys chewing bootlaces, walking with friends, and reminding Melinda that all the best books have a corgi in them.

Ancient Faith Publishing hopes you have enjoyed and bene-fited from this book. The proceeds from the sales of our books only partially cover the costs of operating our nonprofit minis-try—which includes both the work of **Ancient Faith Publishing** and the work of **Ancient Faith Radio**. Your financial support makes it possible to continue this ministry both in print and online. Donations are tax-deductible and can be made at **www.ancientfaith.com.**

To view our other publications,
please log onto our website: **store.ancientfaith.com**

 ANCIENT FAITH RADIO

Bringing you Orthodox Christian music, readings, prayers, teaching, and podcasts 24 hours a day since 2004 at
www.ancientfaith.com